I0734663

Guitar Concerto in C Flat Major, Op. 12: Lucina

S. Morgan Burbank

Iocusia Press

Guitar Concerto In C Flat Major, Op. 12: Lucina, a novella

Published by Iocusia Press, a division of Job at Place LLC, PO Box 256, North Olmsted, OH, 44070

©2025

Paperback ISBN: 978-1-7353190-8-7

Digital ISBN: 978-1-7353190-7-0

Spine and back cover art by Lauren Restivo

Edited by C. Laidig

Front cover art by S. Morgan Burbank

This book is a work of fiction. Names, characters, places, and incidents are fictional. Except for the cats. All cats can be willed into existence if you believe in yourself and you're willing to knock things off of counters. Any resemblance to actual persons, living or dead, companies, events, locations, or politicians is purely coincidental. Any resemblance to actual cats is, however, intentional.

Contents

To those who never seem to get in the place where they belong

Movement 1: Adagio Lamentoso

I hate the Guy gets Girl movie. Why waste an hour and a half doing cool spy shit, saving the world, playing football, or whatever else the film is ostensibly about if Generic Young Actress always ends up in Stock Dudebro's arms? The hopeless romantics are there for the romance. Others are there for the eye candy. Movie studios know that they need a little something for everyone, but it's so overdone. And they always forget one critical reality of love stories.

Not every happy moment has a happy ending if you keep telling the story.

All I wanted to do that Thursday night was to go to the bar with my friend, watch whatever hockey game was on, then go home and enjoy the first three-day weekend I'd had in months. The beauty of overworking yourself is also the tragedy of it. On one hand, you're so exhausted from talking to people that you never want to speak to anyone again. On the other hand, I got to make bank for nearly a year - anything to keep my mind off yet another break-up. A bad one.

I should have known that wasn't how the night would play out. The right time to go home would have been when my buddy's wife called at 8:15 — the handle had broken off their toilet — come home and help her fix it. If he hadn't have left, none of this would have happened.

There's an unmistakable smell that bars have. It's a combination of cheap beer, the general scent of alcohol, and desperation. Mix in a dash or two of whatever food coming out of the kitchen, a whiff of cigarette smoke as some of the regulars come back in from outside, and occasionally whatever vile happenings are going on in the bathroom, and you've got most bars. I will give The Hole in the Wall credit for one thing — and it's not their name. Their chicken wings aren't bad. Boneless of course, saves them forty percent of what you pay on bones. But for a bar, it's good food.

What you do not smell, at least not unless you're throwing back shots of a certain brand of whiskey, is cinnamon. It was so out of place that I had to look away from the game. I had no control over this action. It was like the Wrigley Company knew exactly how to get my attention, painstakingly crafting a powerful cinnamon scent that could break my concentration so thoroughly that I would need to be dead not to find its source.

Being decidedly not dead, I turned my head until I found it. And that's when I knew I was in trouble.

"Excuse me," she said, chewed red gum resting in her cheek as she spoke. "Can I place a food order here?"

"Sure, sweetheart," replied the bartender, Ed. "Now whaddaya want?"

I've known Ed Milton for the better part of a decade now. He's not exactly the best with women. Or men. Or humans. It's not that he's a bad bartender. It's that he just wants you to place your order and move on so he can get to the next customer. The specials are the same every week, yet inevitably someone will ask him what they are. If it's a regular, he's pretty snarky about it. He'll give a newbie a pass as they don't know the place. But you get one pass. That's it.

The fact that she's getting a pass at all is what catches me off guard. I've seen this woman before. Several times. Yet Ed's treating her like it's the first time he's ever talked to her. Come to think of it, I don't think I've ever heard her speak either. She has a nice voice though. Melodic. Soothing.

"Roast beef on rye and some mozzarella sticks," she replied. "And no sugar cola if you've got it."

"Comes with chips," Ed mumbled, already beginning to fill a glass with ice and cola. "Can't replace the chips with the mozzarella sticks. They're separate."

"That's fine," she said. "Will it be ready by nine? Or should I put the order in later?"

"You gonna pass out if you don't eat right away?"

"I'll be fine."

"Come back when you're ready to eat then. Take your soda though."

Ed rolled his eyes at the sound of a glass hitting the floor at the opposite end of the bar. He instinctively whipped the towel off his shoulder as he walked away, sure to give some drunk an earful for breaking shit before the late games started.

I feel compelled to talk to her. Not in the see a pretty girl at the bar all alone and buy her a drink way, but in the broad, the universe is telling me that I need to way. I shouldn't. That's not why I'm here. I have beers to drink and hockey to watch. Both of which still sound good. Yet the more I try to resist speaking to her, the more I want to do just that.

"50/50 shot that he's going to go tell the kitchen to make your food now and it'll be ice cold when you want it," I said.

She looks over at me, a soft smile making its way across her face. Not my typical experience with talking to strangers. Her eyes treat me like I'm an old friend who she hasn't seen in years rather than the weird guy with unkempt hair sipping light beer. I'm suddenly nervous. Does she know me? Do I know her and can't remember who she is? I'm about to embarrass myself, aren't I?

"I don't think so," she replied. "I trust him. Never let me down on mozzarella sticks before."

"You know Ed?"

She laughed. One of those quiet laughs that someone does when they're trying not to disrupt everyone around them. Did I say something stupid?

She smiled and stuck her hand out to me.

"Lucy Ward."

"Daniel Howard," I said, returning her handshake.

"Any chance you're sticking around long enough to listen? I don't have anyone here I know tonight. I want to know how I sound."

"You could ask Ed."

"I'm sure his feedback will be something along the lines of 'ya did good kid, here's your cut, next time bring people with you who'll drink'."

I chuckled then took a sip of my beer.

"Sure you haven't been here before?" I asked. "You've got Ed down already."

"I just know the type," Lucy said. "I can tell a lot about someone by the way they talk."

"Ed's not a particularly complex man. You can read him like a book, but you'll be reading Go Dog, Go."

Lucy smiled and grabbed the glass off the bar, turning on her heel and walking away.

"Talk to you after my set," she said.

Ending a bad relationship is never pleasant, regardless of circumstances. Worse is one fraught with abuse and distrust. But when you're the man being abused by the woman… One phone call to the wrong police station, and you'll have an old dude laughing his ass off while telling you to 'be a man'.

I got out. It took longer than I wanted. Contingencies upon contingencies I had to plan for, money to save. But I got out. Three years, eight months, and counting. And I'm grateful for that.

The funny thing about abuse is that even after the person is out of your life — presuming you're lucky — is how their actions linger on your subconscious. In my case, I couldn't trust. I couldn't believe that someone would treat me kindly without ulterior motives. It's a real kick to the gut to realize that your idea of a happy ending has been warped by someone else's idea of what they wanted to control.

Never chase the girl. No one gets hurt that way.

I zoned out as the game I was watching went to intermission. The wings were fine. The beer was — well, it's beer. Even good beer isn't that good. I absentmindedly scrolled through my phone waiting for the game to come back when a bright guitar chord rang out from the stage.

So who's that girl there?
I wonder what went wrong

The song choice caught my attention. You don't typically see a solo musician on guitar with a computer drum track play Arctic Monkeys. It was nostalgic for me in a way; from a time before everything went to shit.

Her voice was melodic and soothing. The song was a good fit for Lucy's contralto tone, particularly its slow, methodical beginning. My mind's ear envisioned her as being someone who would sing long, emotional ballads. Instead, she opened her set with a song about prostitution. Bold choice.

Then the song's tempo picked up. I think. My body knew that it had. I could hear it but my brain wasn't processing the song. It was like there was a swimming pool between us, the sound fighting through the water in order to get to me. If it weren't for what I was seeing, I would have been convinced I was having a stroke.

Watching her perform was mesmerizing. More than beauty, or the charisma of someone doing what they do best on stage. It was as if her entire visage was calling to me. Her long, ginger hair frantically thrashed about as she jumped along with the beat of the song. Her shoulders, slightly bared from the top she was wearing, sloped like they were cut from a fine marble. Her legs, clad in pale-tinted tights, rose from the black flats on her feet all the way to the swaying black and white houndstooth skirt around her waist.

She was breathtaking. Yet what I was feeling in this moment wasn't just attraction. It felt magnetic. And, in a way, familiar. I was being drawn to her like I needed to learn more but, somehow, like I already knew all there was to know. I didn't need to speak it into existence.

But why? I'd seen her around the bar before, sure. I hadn't talked to her before tonight. I think. Yet, when she told me her name was Lucy, I knew that sounded right. Some people do look very much like the name they're given. But this feeling… It feels like this has happened before.

I do my best to snap out of my train of thought and look around me. It doesn't work. Part of why I come here when I'm stressed is to relax. The background noise of people talking, sports on TV, and games of pool declutters my brain better than most any therapist ever has. I make an effort not to drink until I'm calmed down. Yet here I am, two beers into my night, panicked and confused.

I look back to the stage, but Lucy was already gone, presumably on a set break. Had I really disassociated for that long?

This was bad.

I called over Ed and hastily paid my tab as I downed a glass of water. I hoped this was the alcohol hitting me, but I knew better. A pretty girl you just met doesn't want to just talk. They never do. I needed to leave, quickly.

I made a beeline for my car. The parking lot was fortunately pretty empty, save for a couple of people at the side of the building having a smoke.

That's it. Something to calm my nerves. I keep a pack in my sunglasses compartment for such situations. I told myself I'd give it up, but that's not what needs to happen right now. This is an emergency.

I couldn't get Lucy out of my head. Yes. Pretty girl pretty. But I've met beautiful women before. What was so special about her? Rubbing my eyes, I ran my fingers through my hair, her own deep red burned into my mind. I've always had a thing for both redheads and musicians, but this is different.

It's something else, it has to be. My hands drop to my hips, feeling the rhythm of each step as I walked. The way she moves, how she holds herself, there's such confidence. I wish I could be so sure of myself. I wish I could be...

I shook off the thought and dug my keys out of my pocket. I leaned into my car and opened the sunglasses compartment.

Empty.

Right. That was my old car. They're in the center console in this one.

Empty.

Fuck. They've got to be somewhere. Glovebox? Weird pocket compartment between my door and the speakers? Under my driver's seat?

No luck.

My therapist taught me breathing techniques. Maybe that would work. What was it? Deep breaths to psych us up, rapid breaths to calm down? That sounds legit.

This is worse. Fuck. They're definitely not in here.

"Are you okay?"

I turned around to see Lucy standing a few feet behind me, leaning up against the car beside mine. I felt my heart jump in my throat.

"You left this at the bar," she said, holding out my wallet. "Ed told me he saw you run out. I'm glad I caught you before you left."

"Oh. Yeah, thanks. I thought that I'd lost it."

No harm in lying about why I was freaking out. She didn't need to know.

"It happens. Lucky I happened to be parked right beside you. Made you much easier to find."

The universe wasn't letting me get away from her.

"Mind if I have a smoke?" she asked. "I don't want it to bother you."

"Could I bum one off you?" I replied. "Thought I had some, but I don't."

She grabbed one of those cheap, thin gas station cigars from her purse and handed it to me, lighting it up before doing the same to her own. She took a long drag off it, breathing out the smoke into the crisp air.

"It's my fiftieth show," she said. "Not exactly a huge milestone, but far further than I ever thought I'd get."

"Congratulations."

"Thanks."

"Catch any of it?"

"A little. You've got a great voice. But you're a damn good guitar player."

I wasn't lying. I did technically hear some of it. I just went into a mental spiral that I haven't been able to unravel shortly after she started.

"I know," she said. "I could be better still. Just figured I'd be somewhere else after 50 shows."

"Like where?" I asked.

"I don't even know. Just not a tiny bar in a tiny town."

"I feel that."

"Sorry. Didn't mean to insult the fact that you're at said tiny bar in said tiny town."

"Don't be," I replied. "I wouldn't be here either if I didn't have to be."

"Are you legally required to go to bars?" she asked. Her question elicited a small chuckle from me.

"I don't think there are court orders for that."

"Probably not."

"I just…"

I trailed off. I wanted to say that I meant that I wouldn't be in this small town either. That I'd move away somewhere, anywhere, else if I could. But that, like so many other things, seemed unattainable.

"I should head back in," Lucy said. "Ed probably has my food ready. I should eat it before it gets cold."

Everything in me knew that I should let her walk away. Fuck, I can't form friendships anymore. Bad things were bound to happen to either them or to me. We'd barely talked for two minutes and I already knew she didn't deserve that.

But despite every part of my knowing better…

"Look, I'm sorry I - could I um - coffee? Some time?"

"Coffee sounds great," Lucy said.

"Cool. I can give you my nu—"

"There's a diner down the road," she said, interrupting me. "The coffee sucks, but it's got good pie."

"You said coffee sounded great."

"I did. But pie sounds better."

With that, Lucy smashed the butt of her cigar against the front tire of her car and started walking back inside. I leaned back into my driver's seat, doing my best to dangle the hand holding the still-lit cigar out of the car the best I could. The smell of smoke permeating the seats of my car was a remnant of an earlier era of my life – one I wasn't eager to dredge memories back up from.

At the age of 20, I fell in love with my abuser. Her name isn't important. I feel now like saying it gives her some semblance of power over me. I'm not going to let that happen again. We were together for seven years, five as boyfriend and girlfriend, two engaged. Had I stayed another nineteen days, we would have been husband and wife. That fact still terrifies me. I was so close to being even more trapped than I'd felt.

In retrospect, I'm convinced I proposed out of fear. Whether it was the fear of being alone, of not being able to support myself without her, of what she'd do to me if I didn't, I made the choice. I made it to survive. Not the best strategic one long term, but it stalled the psychological warfare for a few months.

It's hard to feel safe when you have to replay your entire relationship through your mind on the regular to make sure you're telling the truth. It's crushing to wake up next to someone who has no remorse for the mistreatment they've directed at you. There were more nights than I could count where I woke up from a dream — one where I was with someone else, somewhere else, at a time before we were committed to each other — only to cry myself back to sleep as my painful reality snored in the bed beside me. I found myself driving a lot more then. As I drove, I smoked. As I smoked, I calmed down. By the time I got back, armed with whatever trivial shopping good I'd been asked to retrieve, I'd be calm. Not safe, not happy, but calm. And sometimes that's all you can ask for.

I snuffed out the cigar on the asphalt of the parking lot beside my car. I know most people just flicked butts into the lot, but I knew that only created more work for Ed. As I carried it to the receptacle at the door, Lucy came bounding out, guitar bag slung over her shoulder.

"You ready?" she asked, her voice more chipper than when we'd chatted before. "I'm hoping they still have some banana cream when we get there."

"You just went back in?" I replied, confused.

"I finished the second half of my set. You've been out here a while."

"There's no way."

"Are you sure you're okay?"

No. I wasn't sure. How long was I in the car? It certainly didn't seem like I was out here for more than a few minutes.

"I think I'm just hungry," I said. "Let's go get pie."

We drove the half mile down the street to the town's roadside diner. I passed this place nearly every day, yet I could count on one hand the number of times I'd gone in. Aside from the employees and a pair of old men playing chess at a booth in the back, we were the only ones here. We took a seat at the counter, prompting the waiter to greet us.

"Whatcha need?" he asked.

"Coffee, light sugar, no cream, and a slice of banana cream pie," Lucy replied.

"And you?"

I hesitated, struck by her order. It was identical to my own.

"Same as her, please."

Lucy pulled her phone out of her pocket and began absentmindedly looking for something on it. Though tempted to do the same, I resisted, instead simply observing her. Something about her didn't seem real, almost ethereal. This wasn't attraction. It's like she's was forged from a place far away from everything I know, yet simultaneously intimately familiar.

"So...you got any pets?"

The question felt awkward leaving my mouth, almost stumbling over the unsaid words asking their own questions in between each syllable. Not that she could read into it. But I could hear them. Deafeningly so.

"Just one," replied Lucy as she looked up from her phone. "It's a cat. Peebles is her name. Always wanted a fish, but I'm afraid Peebles will eat it."

"I've got a cat. Wanna see a picture?"

"Yes!"

I pulled out my phone and found a picture of a gray Maine Coon cat, laying on my couch asleep one morning.

"Oh my god, it's so adorable!" Lucy squeaked. "I love really fluffy cats. What's its name?"

"This is Otis. He's an asshole. But he's my asshole, so I keep him around."

"Cats are allowed to be like that. They don't know better."

"I'm pretty sure he knocks glasses onto the floor intentionally," I replied. "Must think they sound fun when they hit the floor."

"He knows it gets your attention," replied Lucy.

The next half hour was filled with the two of us trading simple, mundane questions poking around the edges of each others' personality. Her favorite color is blue, favorite pizza topping is ham, favorite drink is rum and cola, favorite season is winter. She'd gone to college for two years, but dropped out to take care of her mom before she died. Lucy and Peebles lived in an apartment in a suburb about 40 minutes away.

As the night wore on, the few other patrons of the diner made their way out, leaving just the two of us alone with the cook and the waitress. Not wanting to have the staff continually worry about us, we paid our tab and made our way out to the parking lot where we both leaned against our respective cars and continued the conversation. A chill on the wind prompted me to throw my jacket around her shoulders, leading to the two of us side-by-side against her car. Our fingertips would occasionally brush the other's hand, but neither of us was assertive enough to act on it.

"I'll have you know I've become quite fond of your company, Daniel."

She turned and faced me. Her face was inches from mine, piercing blue-green eyes cutting through my soul and sapping my strength until my knees threatened to buckle under me. Even after coffee and dinner, I could still smell the lingering scent of her cinnamon gum on her breath.

"I quite enjoy yours too."

I caught the faintest sight of electric blue nail polish blurring by my eyes as she wrapped her arms around my neck. In the split second before her lips touched mine, I panicked. Is this an elaborate setup? Will she rob me? Why not any of the muscled-up construction workers that frequented the bar? This is going too well, it didn't make any sense.

Then we kissed. And my brain shut the fuck up.

And that was the problem.

I pulled myself away and walked to the other side of the parking lot, pacing between two lampposts. I could hear her dumbfounded stare screaming behind me.

I hate that we're in public. Her car was between me and my car. If I tried to make a break for it, we'd have to cross paths eventually. I could sprint through the woods. That would eliminate the problem of going past her. Unfortunately, I have no sense of direction, no flashlight, and no survival skills. Not exactly the prerequisites you want to be missing in a place you don't know.

"Just a hug then?"

I don't know how I didn't hear her come up behind me. I nodded. She wrapped her arms around me and pulled back into her, giving me the tightest embrace I'd had since I was a child.

It was at that moment I lost it.

I don't remember how we ended up back at our cars or how quickly she got me there. All I recall of that part of the evening was crying into her cardigan — and when that got too wet, her shoulder. In between cries, I babbled out bits and pieces of my past. I'm sure I sounded crazy, especially for a first date. The manipulation, the control, the fear – it all came flooding back. And yet, she didn't leave.

By the time I finally calmed myself, it was well past two in the morning.

"I'm sorry I kept you here this long," I said. "I'm a mess."

"Don't apologize," replied Lucy. "You needed someone."

"A psychiatrist," I mumbled.

"While I do think there would be benefits to therapy," she countered, "that doesn't mean I won't listen."

I leaned my head against Lucy's shoulder, not wanting to look at her as I shared my next thought.

"I'm… I'm not ready for a relationship," I said. Before she had the chance to respond, I quickly continued on. "And it's not you. You're…incredible. Gorgeous. Being a musician doesn't hurt."

"Totally the reason I got into music," she snarked.

"I'm mad at myself for not staying."

"Don't be. If you want, I can get my acoustic out of my trunk and sing to you."

Lucy ran her fingers through my hair. I couldn't tell you the last time someone had done that. I immediately melted into her embrace, content. For the first time in a long time, I didn't feel alone.

Then, it went dark. A sense of dread in my chest.

I shot up from my resting position, darkness enveloping all of my senses. I looked around, but Lucy was gone. I flailed around, trying to reach my phone that I knew I left on top of my car. The first attempt missed everything, leaving me with a feeling of falling through the air. My second reach hit wood. I lunged again, this time smacking my elbow hard.

It wasn't the car.

I went silent and listened to the world around me.

All I could hear was intermittent snoring coming from the other side of the bed.

I laid back down and started to cry.

Movement 2: Allegro Con Grazia

This isn't the kind of place I ever saw myself ending up. Drug dealers and thieves end up waiting on the docks in the middle of the night, not middle managers at a marketing firm. Why I was there isn't technically illegal, at least not right now. The only person likely to get upset about this was my wife. With any luck, by the time this is all sorted out, there won't be a need for her to get angry with me ever again.

There are above the table ways to have an artificially intelligent being created. In most countries, it's as simple as finding a manufacturer who's selling an android with the features you're looking for, then plugging in a simulation or personality module you want. A few thousand dollars later, it's yours. There are high-end models with advanced programming capable of helping you run a business, raising your children, or even living off the grid. Hell, there was an entire kind of robot based on generated personalities from dating websites. It got pretty big here for a decade or so, which is also why so many who are stuck in their ways lobbied to kill off the practice. Only God can create life. Only God can create love. It was just another hate-filled slogan wrapped in family-friendly paper made by people whose only desire was to cling to a power they weren't actually losing.

It was just past 10:45pm according to the $8 watch I bought that night. I watched as a few snowflakes fell in front of the lone streetlamp in my line of sight. It was a little early in the year for snow, but it's kind of pretty when it doesn't stick to anything. The car supposed to pick me up was running late. Shady people aren't exactly known for their promptness. Even the name of the person I was supposed to see sounded fake. You can't expect me to believe there's a person whose government name is Penny Australia. It doesn't matter to me, so long as they help me to get what I want and stay quiet about it. But come on. At least make up a semi-plausible fake name.

I wished I had my phone with me. But the advice I was given – advice I intended to follow – was to leave everything that could be tracked at home. No phone, no credit card, no smart wear, nothing. I'm sure they'd gone over that same explanation with however many people sought out the totally real Dr. Penny Australia in the past. Most people don't think about how their every move, every action, and every thought could be used against them, not to mention how easy it is for those same things to be easily tracked.

I wish I didn't know.

I stare into the night sky, clouds obscuring the heavens above from my view. I'd be able to see Jupiter and Mars if they weren't there – Pluto's up there somewhere too, even if my naked eye could never find it. Instead of the celestial beauty of the universe, I'm stuck with the nagging feeling that somehow, someway, all the precautions I've taken tonight won't be good enough. And then I'll be accused of something

– anything – far more heinous than what I've actually done. There's precedent for it. Not that I wish to relive those moments.

At five minutes after eleven, a lone gray sedan with darkly tinted windows made its way down the lane and into the dockyard. It circled once before pulling up beside me. The rear passenger window rolled down, allowing me to see a middle-aged blonde man in a white suit sitting on the opposite side of the car.

"Your name?" he said, his voice thick, nearly growling.

"Daniel Howard," I replied. I'd considered giving them a fake name, but I thought better of it. Something tells me they would have found out who I was anyway.

"Get in."

The car ride was silent, save for occasional sighs come from the blonde man as he stared at his phone. From the dim light of the screen, I could see that he was frustrated with whatever was happening. Maybe he was annoyed he was here with me instead of home with a plate of nachos watching the game.

"Detroit fan?" I asked, trying to chip away at his icy demeanor. He didn't even blink.

This guy must meet people all the time who he picks up for shady dealings. He probably thinks I'm going to go buy a robot to fuck it. I get that people do that. Hell, I don't even fault them for it. But it's not why I'm doing this. If it was only about sex, I could head back home and assume the baby-making position as is expected of me. No. This is for an emotional connection to something – someone.

She's been cheating for years. I know it. It's not like she does a particularly good job of hiding it. I wouldn't be shocked if she wanted me to find out, file for divorce, that way the blame for the separation is on me. I'm fairly sure she knows I know. At this point, cut the pretense. If she can cheat freely, I can make a friend. Literally.

After a half hour or so, we came to a stop. The man motioned for me to get out of the car, barely looking up from his phone in doing so. I'd expected to be in a run down, dark area of the city, much like the one we'd just come from. But instead of another series of docks along the Detroit River, I found myself on the front steps of a mansion in Grosse Pointe Shores. For someone who was so willing to the terms of secrecy we'd mutually agreed upon for our meeting, this was quite the audacious choice of venue.

At the front door of the building was a butler in a blue suit. He held the door open for me, muttering a greeting all the while. Despite this, he refused to make eye contact with me, barely even looking at me beyond ensuring I was through the door before he shut it. It felt like he was ashamed of me being here for me – like the mere fact that I was taking this meeting somehow made me not even worthy to cast his eyes on.

A cheery, slightly musical voice rang out. "A good evening to you, Mr. Howard."

I hate and love the fact that I can remember the first dream I had about Lucy. She was this ray of sunshine for my mind, lighting me up after what had been a particularly sour night. I thank my subconscious every day for showing her to me, as my waking brain could have never come up with someone so perfect for what I wanted and needed out of life.

The downside was that I woke up to my wife trying to smother me with a pillow. She initially said it was because I was snoring. She later admitted it was because I'd called out her name – Lucy – while dreaming. Three weeks later, my wife bought a new pillow and bedroom set. Nothing had ever happened. Or so I'm told.

From the far end of the hallway, Dr. Penny Australia began her swift walk toward me. She was much younger than she'd sounded on the phone – in her mid-30s at the oldest – wearing a dark blue suit matching that of the butler and sparkling pumps that twinkled in the light as she walked. There's no way she'd wear something like this around if a potential client weren't here, yet the grandeur of the mansion did give me pause to wonder.

"Please," she continued, "come to the parlor. I'll have Aurelie bring us some drinks. There's much to discuss."

I followed her into a sprawling room with several seating areas around various smaller tables. The room was decorated with a litany of cubist art. Though I was certain none of the works were actual Picassos or Le Fauconniers, I couldn't rule it out. Aside from the paintings, there were bookshelves filled with leather bound books, the scent of dusty cowhide mixing with the aroma of rich mahogany and a faint trace of a lingering cigar to transport the environment back one hundred years or more. Hell of a place to sign some paperwork. The aura alone is intimidating.

Dr. Australia took a seat on a bright red chaise lounge that faced out a window overlooking the river. She motioned for me to take a seat in one of the nearby chairs, giving me a view of the night sky facing toward Canada. Before I'd fully settled, a maid placed glasses of water near us.

"Thank you," said Penny. "I'll have a spritz. What can Aurelie bring you, Mr. Howard?"

"Daniel, please," I said. "I'll be fine with water."

"Nonsense. It's not a proper meeting unless it's over drinks. I'm happy to order for you if you're indecisive."

I debated sticking to my guns. I'd only made it this far into my plan by staying as clear headed as I could. My glance caught Aurelie's, drawing me into her gaze. Her eyes begged for me to make a choice. It was as if she was silently calling out to me that she wanted me to make a choice

– or at the very least that she didn't want to have to make two trips after I spent too long thinking my drink order over.

"Negroni, please," I said.

Aurelie gave me a quick smile, then turned on her heels and left the room. Once the door shut behind her, Dr. Australia broke the silence.

"An interesting choice for your order," she said.

"I mean, I like gin and bitters," I said. "Can't go wrong mixing them together."

"That's not what I meant. Most people I meet with want to try out the wares first thing before committing to buying. If they're unsure of themselves and their – shall we say, performance – it's usually a couple shots of tequila. You chose a sipping drink. Your mind is made up."

"I'm sorry. Try out the wares?"

"You didn't even notice, did you?"

I shook my head.

"Aurelie is one of our creations," Penny said. "When she comes back, take a look at her. Really examine her. I'm sure you'll find our craftsmanship and our technology to be superb."

"I'm not here to buy a sex doll," I replied.

"Of course not. Most of my clients aren't coming here looking for something to fuck. Not exclusively, that is. Companionship is what I deal in, Mr. Howard. The programs and personas I create are meant to allow you to develop deep emotional connections first and foremost. The fact that there are extra benefits that come with that is merely a bonus. Think of it like the extra fries you find in the bag when you get your hamburger."

Aurelie returned to the room, drinks in hand. She placed Dr. Australia's drink on the coffee table in front of her, then made her way over to place my negroni on the end table beside me. As she moved closer, I noticed for the first time that she wore no shirt beneath her blue suit jacket. Her hand briefly touched my own as she pulled away from the glass. I'd heard countless times that android skin was clammy to the touch or unsettlingly plastic to look at. But the touch of her fingertips and the brief glance at her chest beneath the jacket proved otherwise.

"Reconsidering?" asked Penny.

"I'm a married man, Dr. Australia," I replied.

"Most of my clients are. Married, that is. You'd be surprised how many of my clients are women looking for something better in their lives. Something that makes them feel more like themselves."

Why word it like that? I just said I'm a married man. I'm not hiding that fact. What's she seeing that I'm not? Did I fill out something on the form that made her think there's more to this than what I'm telling her? I tried to be as vague as possible.

She slid closer to me, her voice no longer the bombastic, confident tone she'd been speaking in. It was like she wanted to be in on my secret. Not just the secret of why I was here, every secret that led me to end up at this point.

"Tell me about her," she said, her voice hushed and soothing.

"You already have all the specs of my request," I replied.

"No. Tell me about who she is. What does she give you that you lack now?"

One of the biggest things that movies and television leaves out about in vitro fertilization is that it doesn't always take. Women go through these arduous counseling and review sessions, appointment after appointment, dollar after dollar spent. And sometimes, pregnancy just doesn't happen. It's not anyone's fault, per se. It could be the woman's age, her eggs, endometriosis - the cause for failure during one round of IVF might not be the same cause for failure the next time.

Of course, none of these matters when what the person you're married to wants more than anything is a baby. And it matters even less when, three years into your marriage to this person who believes it's their God-given destiny to be a mother, you learn that you're sterile.

"Well, she –"

"Start with her name," Penny interrupted.

"Her name's Lucy," I said. "Lucina technically, but Lucy for short."

"Are you modeling her after someone? Is she a real person?"

"What?" I replied, shocked at the accusation. "Why would someone create an android of a real person?"

"Some people want to revive the visage of a dead relative or spouse," she replied. "People deal with grief in different ways. Lucy could have been an ex-girlfriend that died in a car crash. Or you could be a creeper trying to make your own version of a girl you met at a bar but struck out with."

"It's nothing like that. She isn't real."

"If you want me to make her real, I need to understand her. She's going to be real when all this is done. Just as real as Aurelie is, if not more so."

I sighed. I'd never expressed where the idea for Lucy had come from out loud to anyone. Certainly not to a stranger.

"Is this backstory really necessary?" I inquired.

"I wouldn't be asking if it weren't," Penny replied. "This is a complicated endeavor for us and an expensive investment for you. We aren't some dating site creating computer programs that people fall in love with. We create real connections. At a bare minimum, the goal is to ensure that you have a friend – a companion – that will be with you for the rest of your life. The more I understand what you're looking for and why, the better your experience will be and the less likely you are to have buyer's remorse. The work we do changes lives, Daniel. Let me change yours."

I took a long sip of my drink, holding the glass in my hands as I let the warmth created by the alcohol coat my soul and steel my resolve.

"I've been in therapy for five years now," I began. "Lucy's a recent development comparatively speaking. She only started appearing to me in the last year or two."

"Appearing?"

"In dreams. Which I know sounds batshit crazy. I'm pretty sure the only reason my therapist still sees me is because I'm paying off her mortgage just because I can't get my shit together."

I stopped myself. This was the kind of talk that my therapist had encouraged me to avoid. I wasn't perfect. But the self-blame for things that weren't my fault was a habit that I'd found hard to break. Of course, if I was to the point where one of my top concerns was whether or not I was following the kind of self-talk that my therapist wanted, this evening has gone far off the deep end. Too late to turn back now though.

"Let me rephrase that," I said. "I've been through my share of challenges. I haven't always reacted the best to them. But I'm working to make myself better despite the circumstances I'm in. My therapist calls the idea of Lucy a coping mechanism. My brain struggles with the reality of my waking life and what it's become. As our sessions focused more on what could be done to make things better, I thought about how my life would be different if…"

I trailed off. I took a moment to contemplate my next statement, wording that had oscillated back and forth between two ideas across the various times I'd discussed my life, my marriage, and my trauma.

A hand came to rest on my shoulder, startling me and causing me to realize I'd begun to stare off into space. Aurelie handed me a tissue, taking a few paces back and standing by the window after I'd accepted it. I wiped away the tear that had begun to form in the corner of my left eye, before folding the tissue up and gripping it in my hand.

"One of the underrated selling points of our work is the ability of our androids to anticipate the needs of a companion," Dr. Australia said. "The technology has come a long way in the past couple of years. Aurelie's abilities are a bit more experimental in nature – she was made to be part of my life after all – allowing her to care for others beyond her companion. I assure you we can mold Lucy into whatever need in your life."

"What do you mean?" I asked.

"That depends on what you want it to mean. I've had people come here for the obvious reasons. The sex. The control. The power. And I hate those kinds of clients, but they help keep the business running. It's much more exciting when I get to work with someone seeking an equal or a helper out of my work. A few months ago, I had a mother come to me about getting an android to work with her disabled son. She'd been his caretaker since birth all the way through early adulthood. But she just learned she's terminally ill and wanted to make sure that there was someone who could care for him as their primary goal – just as it had been hers through life.

"That's the kind of story that makes the work I do fulfilling. I only get one of those for every twenty rich fuckheads I work with. But whether it's someone trying to make sure their child is cared for, a person trying to create a safety net to escape a bad relationship, or a elderly individual wanting to make sure they have someone to spend their final days with, it's the not shitty people worth helping."

***

One of the hardest things to do as a human, at least according to my therapist, is to find comfort and acceptance in living with decisions that may not initially be of our own making, but that are reinforced by our decision to live with their outcome. I watched my father go through this himself as I grew up. I know he didn't want children. I overheard the arguments he had with my mother late at night. But he stayed. He loved me and my sisters. He refused to put us through the same challenges he'd faced growing up in a broken home. So he stayed with my mother until I, the youngest child of three, had graduated high school. He served her with divorce papers the day after my graduation party.

I never used to think he'd made a smart choice. The idea of two Christmases and countless Friday and Sunday evenings spent traversing between homes seemed ideal, so long as everyone was happy. My sisters might not have agreed, but to me, all I wanted was my parents to stay together, even after I was old enough to realize that they weren't good together. Even though I understood why he didn't leave, that didn't mean I agreed with his choice.

Love can change a person, both for better and for worse. Unfortunately, so can a single-minded determination to get what you want at the cost of the happiness of others. You either leave the relationships around you burnt to the ground, destroying everyone else but yourself, or you learn to compromise. We can't always have what we want in life.

***

"What's her personality like, Daniel?" Dr. Australia asked again. "We can work through the looks and what not after. That comes easier to most people. The personality is what matters most."

I closed my eyes, trying to summon the emotions that Lucy brought to my slumbering mind. Describing how the idea of Lucy made a conscious version of me feel was easy. I yearned for her support. I longed for her compassion. I craved her kindness. But telling anyone that would make me sound crazy – and it wouldn't do Lucy justice. Then again, I had revealed that my goal was to purchase an android that took the personification of my dream-induced coping mechanism for domestic abuse. I'm certain that anything that came out of my mouth would be fine.

"Have you ever curled up in a soft blanket that's fresh out of the dryer?" I asked.

Fuck. That didn't sound any saner.

"I mean, her voice is that soothing," I said. "It's calming to hear her talk. I can go to bed and spend hours in bed battling with these massive anxiety spirals, wondering if I'd remember what happened that day well enough that it couldn't be used against me tomorrow. But then I'd hear her. She makes waking up just a bit better, even if she isn't there.

"I don't know what it is. It's one thing to wake up one morning and realize you love someone else. People fall out of love, grow apart. But I'm lying in bed at three in the morning, and I'm realizing the person I'm supposed to share a life with is…views me as a way to achieve their own gains. And all I can do, all my brain can do, is create these fragments of an alternate life with a fake person who is the exact opposite of your spouse in every way that's important to me. I feel broken."

"Then why us?" asked Dr. Australia. "Why not divorce your wife? Or seek out different therapy to help calm this dream reality?"

As problems in our marriage began to mount, I told a friend about my concerns with my wife. Infidelity is understood to be a thing that can go both ways in a relationship. I've known that my wife has been cheating on me for a couple of years now. While I don't think the sterility diagnosis caused it explicitly, it certainly accelerated the fact that it was inevitable to happen.

Robbie. Not Rob or Bob. Not Robert. Not even Bobby. Robbie. With an ie. I don't know why that got to me so much when I found out. For the longest time, I thought she was just using him like she was me. The key difference between me and Robbie, aside from the fact that he's 10 years younger than me, hot, and has that sweet, sweet trust fund money, is that his sperm isn't all dead. In my mind, all he was to her was a dick and balls. Between Robbie and the IVF, something had to work.

It hasn't. And it is unfortunate. Despite my own hatred for how everything has played out over our marriage, I still want her to be happy. I know that's a terrible thing to say all things considered, but when you love someone, you want them to be happy. It's why I didn't say anything when I found out she was banging Beachbod Bonerpants. It's why I agreed to spend thousands of dollars we'd been saving to go on a trip to Europe on IVF. It's why I took on extra shifts at work. I might have been a doormat, but I was doing it for the right reasons. At least I thought so.

I'm glad I got the money out when I did. Filtering money out of a bank account slowly over time. I had longer to feel guilty, but at least it was guilt I was feeling. It was a welcome change from normal.

"I want…no, I need, someone who make me feel hope in my life again."

"Hope for what?" Dr. Australia asked.

"Myself," I replied. "For the person I've always wanted to be and never been able to."

We began to hammer out the details of what Lucy's persona would be like. She'd be charming and flirtatious, outgoing, and forward. Lucy would love pets and children, though neither would be dealbreakers for her if they weren't in her life. She'd have musicianship skills that only showed up in one dream, if only as a selfish request on my part due to my own attraction to women who can sing and play music. Beneath it all though, she'd be kind, compassionate, and caring.

When it came time to work out the details of how Lucy would look, I struggled more than I'd expected. Her pale skin juxtaposed against her burnt sienna hair was seared into my subconscious, though it did take me longer than I'd hoped to explain that burnt sienna was, in fact, a shade of ginger hair, not brown. Her eyes seemed to change between gray, silver, green, and blue in my dreams with no rhyme or reason, much the same way as she varied in height from being well shorter than me to slightly taller. In the end, the only things I settled on were the complexion, her hair color, and general body type, leaving the rest up to Dr. Australia to build as she so desired.

As we were finishing up, I laid out the last, critical request that I had.

"I need to be sure that Lucy, despite being designed and created by me, will still be able to make choices about her own autonomy. I don't want her to be forced into being attached to me."

"All of our androids have some amount of free will," Dr. Australia replied.

"I'm not asking for her to have some amount of free will," I replied. "I want someone who will give me the chance to prove myself to them as a friend, and then from there, whatever may come shall come. If it's romantic, great."

"You do realize that going barhopping would be a significantly cheaper way to achieve that, right? It's a lot of money for there to be no guarantee she'll stick around."

"What's the alternative?"

"We typically have some level of failsafe coding where an android will remain loyal to the person who acquired it," she said. "So long as they're not being abusive or causing physical danger to the android, the android will remain loyal. There are some companies who have chosen to give their androids or computer programs full free will. And while that's noble of them, I don't view it as a particularly sound investment for my clients."

"Can Aurelie leave?" I asked.

"Aurelie is well-cared for and respected," Dr. Australia replied. "She and Reginald, the butler android you met when you got here, take care of my needs and I, in turn, take the best care of them that I can."

"That doesn't answer my question."

Aurelie had been lingering in the back of the room for the entirety of our conversation, ready to act on any request that Penny made. She stared at Dr. Australia waiting for her answer. If she was concerned about what would come out of her creator's mouth, her expression didn't show it. After the silence lingered on far longer than I felt comfortable with, the android finally spoke up, albeit in a soft voice.

"Penny," said Aurelie. "Please answer him."

"Should they ever desire to leave me, I would not stop them," replied Penny. "They do have coding that makes them loyal to me and does discourage them from leaving. However, if it's what they truly wanted, I would not stop them."

"And you don't think this is a problem?" I asked. "You've given a creation free will, yet force them to follow you or else?"

"I said discourage, Mr Howard, not force. My goal is to create the best artificially intelligent beings that I'm capable of while not running afoul of the law. I absolutely could give an android complete free will. It would be the right thing to do. But I'm not looking to get shut down like RobotixWares or Project Freyja. And when you live somewhere run by a group of people who can't accept love between an android and a human, yet actively encourages humans to own those same robots — many of whom are far more intelligent, compassionate, and human than the very people who own them – you put in necessary failsafes to cover your own ass. It's not about playing God. It's about protecting myself, my clients, and most importantly, my creations from those who wish to play God for themselves. Therefore, I encourage you to reconsider not having a failsafe, both for your protection and for Lucy's."

★★★

"Always the victim."

I took the car back to the docks. Penny told me that a second car would be there waiting to take me back to the office, wherein I'd pick up my car and drive home. It was past two in the morning by the time I pulled into my driveway. The best-case scenario would be going into my house, not disturbing our easily startled dog, crawling into bed, and no one being the wiser until morning. It'd lead to some awkward conversations about why I'd agreed to take on an overnight shift at work and didn't bother to wake her when I got home. But I was equipped to deal with those.

"It never happened like that, stop blowing things out of proportion."

More realistically, she'd be mad. She'd be pissed. It'd be this whole thing that I'd end up apologizing for repeatedly. Then, in a few weeks, when she'd tell me she went to strip club with her friends, when she was making out with one of her female co-workers, or whatever other story came to light, I'd be told I was overreacting. That I needed to let her have her freedom. In a sense, I was. The whole point to tonight was to give myself the freedom to let someone else be everything I needed from her. The lack of physical satisfaction wasn't changing, but fortunately, the internet is still for porn.

"It's always my fault right? If I'm such a horrible wife why are you still here?"

31

The entirety of all three car rides, I could hear my wife's words going through my head. All things I'd heard for years, all statements I couldn't get out of my mind no matter how much time and effort I could ever spend doing so. I thought that would make this easy. The idea of bringing the person who was her antithesis into my life was such an obvious one. It's exactly what I needed.

"Your friends? Real friends don't tell you to leave your wife."

And yet, here I was questioning if I'd done the right thing. Who thought it was a good idea to give humanity the power to create life in any capacity, let alone one that's beyond our own mortal means? Was I being no better than she was by doing this? Even if my intentions were good, were my actions the same in practice?

"I'm selfish? When you're a dad, you're gonna have to learn to put someone else before you for a change."

The dog didn't bark when I came in the door. In fact, nothing made a sound at all when I came in. After several hours of nervous discussion and a few drinks, I needed to relieve myself, sneaking into the upstairs bathroom and turning on the shower light.

That's when I noticed the medicine cabinet's door hanging open – and the inside empty save for my toothbrush and contact case.

I snuck around the house. It was oddly quiet.

There was a note on the counter. She'd left to be with Robbie. How he'd finally given her what I never could. How unmanly I was for failing her so many times. How unhappy I'd be without her – and how much I deserved it all for how I'd treated her.

She was gone. The dog, everything in the kitchen, damn near everything in the bathroom and our bedroom too. All that was left was my clothes, my toiletries, and half-empty two liter of Mountain Dew. And Otis – the grumpy old cat who we'd adopted because he kept showing up on our doorstep beginning for food. At least he's still here.

I crumpled to the ground in the middle of my kitchen and began to laugh. It started slow and quiet, building to a loud, cackling crescendo.

It was finally over.

★★★

Four weeks later, I woke up to the sound of a knock at my front door. I clumsily stumbled out of bed, throwing on a pair of shorts left on the floor for an indeterminate amount of time, along with a t-shirt from the top of a hamper. I'd taken the week off from work to sort out the paperwork from the annulment, not to mention meeting with lawyers far more than I'd otherwise have liked to. I'd made it to Friday though. I was no longer married. And yet someone felt the need to interrupt my day for sleeping in.

I groggily grabbed a bottle of pre-made iced coffee from the fridge as I made my way to the door. Even if the caffeine wouldn't kick in this quickly, if it was someone important, I had to look like my tired ass was trying to wake up. And if it was someone trying to sell me something, I had something to throw at them. Best of both worlds.

I opened the door to Dr. Penny Australia standing on my welcome mat. She wore the same blue suit as the night we'd met, though it shimmered more in the early morning sun than it had under her home's artificial lighting. Aurelie flanked her from behind, holding a box of donuts.

"I didn't order breakfast," I grumbled, taking a sip of my coffee.

"You can't meet someone for the first time without drinks or food," said Dr. Australia. "And since it's socially unacceptable to have scotch before noon, we brought breakfast."

"I chose donuts!" Aurelie added excitedly.

"And Lucy?" I asked.

"We'll bring her in momentarily," Penny replied. "It'd be best to make good first impression. Do you have anything less…casual?"

"I'm lucky I still have this. Anything that wasn't work clothes got wiped out when she left."

"I see. Aurelie. Please arrange for Reginald to take Daniel shopping for whatever he needs. On us."

Before I could speak, Aurelie was already out the door and out of earshot.

"That's really not necessary," I said.

"Think of it as a perk for being a loyal customer," she replied. "Lucy was no small investment, and divorces are--. I may be running a business, but I'm not heartless."

The front door opened again, Aurelie leading in a tall, slender redhead in a purple hoodie with gray sleeves and black leggings. Lucy smiled as she saw me, like an old friend you haven't seen in years crossing paths with you in the grocery store.

"Hi," she said, her voice sending fluttering sensations throughout my entire body. "I'm Lucy. I'm so happy I finally get to meet you."

My dream girl was standing before me.

"It's been a long time coming," I said.

She looked every bit what I envisioned in my head. It was like looking into a mirror.

As Aurelie unpacked paper plates from a bag and handed them to each of us, Dr. Australia talked to Lucy, setting expectations of her transition to living with me. In four weeks, I'd gone from living in a total nightmare to having the literal girl of my dreams standing in front of me. Everything was perfect.

Too perfect.

Movement 3: Largo Ma Non Troppo

Fuck alarm clocks. They're a good idea in theory. A piece of machinery wakes you up when you need to get up. The problem isn't the tool rather what it represents. We live in a society where the needs of the many do not outweigh the needs of the few. And the few control the means to existence to such an extent they present their collective goals as an overarching monolith to which we are all beholden. So, in order to pay my bills and live comfortably, I need to be a morning person. For the economy. It demands so little of us while giving so much in return. Pretty sure that's the slogan.

I could hear sounds of life in the house already. Lucy's pouring food into Otis's bowl. He's probably darting around her legs, happily purring that someone is giving him food. Probably doesn't hurt that she's not grumpy about it either.

Lucy was everything I dreamed her to be and more. She's compassionate. She's caring. She's breathtaking. She's witty. And she was here, happily living with me. This was what I wanted. I'd been through Hell.

Not only did I come out the other side, paradise was waiting for me when I got there.

So why couldn't I get out of bed? Why was the alarm clock – already one of my least favorite inventions of modern society – an even more prominent harbinger of doom?

"Daniel?" Lucy's melodic voice rang out from the other side of the bedroom door. "Are you up?"

I closed my eyes, taking a moment to compose my thoughts. Deep breath in. Out slowly.

"Yeah," I mumbled, trying my best to sound half asleep.

"Would you like breakfast? I can make something."

"I'll do it after I shower."

"Are you sure?"

"Yeah."

I laid there for a moment, waiting for the sounds of Lucy's footsteps to let me know she wasn't right outside. Once I was certain she was gone, I grabbed my outfit for the day and made my way to the bathroom. I'd long held the habit of taking my work clothes to the bathroom with me while I showered – a holdover from my post-college laziness where that's how I steamed the wrinkles out of them. Lately this served the sole purpose of giving me a sense of ease. It was my house and she was an android. Didn't make it feel right to walk around naked without her consent.

The water from the showerhead quickly filled up the room with steam, obscuring the mirrors and matching the fog inside my own brain. I didn't want to go to work. As I stepped into the shower, I debated my options. I could call off now, but then I'm still at home with the source of my anxiety. I could leave first then take the day, but I'd have to commit to being out of the house until my workday ends. I don't like people that much. Or I could just go to work. The downside to that was clearly work. The upside?

I'd chosen not to listen to Dr. Australia about the failsafe protocols. Lucy didn't need one. She deserved the chance to be her own person, whatever that meant. I couldn't let her be like Reginald or Aurelie. Humans shouldn't have ownership over other humans. And since Lucy fit the bill of a human in every sense of the word except for her physical makeup, I reasoned that courtesy extended to her as well. I'm positive I did the right thing in making that choice.

But in doing the right thing for someone else, was I setting myself up for failure? I couldn't hold one marriage together. Every attempt at dating I'd ever made prior to that failed spectacularly, hence ending up where I did. What made me think this was going to go any better?

And who was to say Lucy would even be interested in me? I understood that she felt some sort of kinship toward me because I made her real. Friendship with Lucy was not in question. She told great stories, she was a charming and funny conversationalist, and above all else, she was kind to me. We had some similar interests – a fact that the programming allowed me to choose – but her innate curiosity outside of those topics made her endlessly captivating to talk to. Lucy was not the problem here.

There were feelings, sure. Objectively, I knew it wasn't love. It was trauma from the divorce. It was finding kindness and hope in another person. It was lust, as I did find her attractive. It was anything and everything but love.

And…something else. Something I'd been fighting and hiding from for years. A shadow that mocked my every move on a sunny day, lurking, mirroring my actions as I went about my business. At first, I found it to be grotesque. It was a source of shame I kept hidden in the darkest recesses of my mind. But over the years, I'd become accepting of its presence, realizing not that it followed me to taunt me, but because it was part of me.

I closed my eyes and let water rush down over my face. I typically hated the feeling of water anywhere near my head, but in this moment, the relentless droplets were calming. Tension released from my head as they pounded the skin around my eyes and nose, large drips forming on the ends of my eyelashes before running down my cheeks. I wasn't getting anything done in this shower. I hadn't touched my soap or shampoo. All the more I could ask for was a therapeutic rinse. Shame what the water was doing for my outside couldn't be applied to the inside.

"Daniel?"

Lucy's voice broke my focus. It was louder and closer than I'd expected.

"Are you okay?" she asked.

I turned and opened my eyes to find her peeking her head in the bathroom door. The steam and dew on the glass door obscured my body from her sight…I think. It'd be enough to stop a human from seeing me. I hadn't thought about the implications for Lucy. Did she have the same ability to see as people did? Or did she have some sort of super sight that only androids could have?

"Daniel? You've been in here almost an hour. Are you alright?"

Fuck. Had it really been that long?

"I'll be alright."

I lied. I wasn't alright. And even though Lucy was trying to help, her presence here was the last thing I needed. She was a reminder of everything I hadn't been able to get away from. The external horrors were gone. But what was left was present in my deepest thoughts, lingering from dusk til dawn and back again. And now, standing before me through misty glass, was the physical manifestation of those idle ideas.

"I'll go make breakfast," she said. "Want me to wait until the water shuts off so I know you're getting out?"

"That's fine," I replied. At least, I think I did. I can't be sure I actually said it out loud. Everything is starting to blur together.

She must have left the room, as the air fell silent save for the rhythmic pounding of water on my body. It was cold – it had been for a while, but it's not like I could do anything to fix that. It takes time for a water heater to refill and that's time where I'd have to talk. To confront what had been in my head this whole time.

It's not that I didn't want to talk to Lucy. I had a million thoughts going through my head. I wanted to tell her how I longed for happiness. For her to be companion who I shared life's ups and downs with. I didn't know if what I wanted was romantic or sexual or whatever and I'd spent weeks after she arrived trying to figure it out, all while getting to know this being that had come into my life at my behest.

At some point in the future, I'd tell her about how I used to dream about her. How I knew her before she ever knew herself. And how bringing her into reality has only caused me to realize how narrow and short-sighted my visions of her were. I get that dreams aren't exactly accurate representations of reality. A clown on a bicycle wouldn't be able to keep up with me driving a stock car if they were. But the differences between dream Lucy and real Lucy were startling. How I'd envisioned her seemed so flat and reductive. She wasn't just the pretty redhead who played music for me at the bar. She was so much more that I didn't know.

And that's exactly the problem. What if I did get to know her and she wasn't the person for me? What if I wasn't the person for her? I'd built her up as this cure-all for my troubles for nothing. Maybe my mind was just imagining someone different, someone better than what I was experiencing firsthand as a way to cope with being belittled, hurt, and abused. And then my arrogant ass, thinking I could play God, brought that idea of a person into the world as nothing more than a conduit for my own insecurities. What a fucking asshole I was.

But. Here's the thing. The most frustrating, agonizing part that I didn't come to realize until after she was already in my home.

The girl in the dream wasn't Lucy. It was me. It was me all along.

I took a long, measured breath in and shut the water off. I grabbed my towel, doing my best not to drip all over the floor as I dried myself off. A faint scent was coming from the kitchen – cinnamon? – overwhelming the smell of steam and body wash that permeated these walls.

The door leading out to my bedroom mocked me. If I stayed in here, so does the problem. No one else has to be burdened with it. If I open the door, my mouth will blurt things out. If not now, eventually. And then it's everyone's problem.

"Daniel?"

Her voice broke my spiral, snapping me back into reality.

"Are you alright?" she asked from the other side of the door. "I made cinnamon rolls and eggs."

"Would you mind leaving so I can get dressed?" I asked. "I'll be out in a minute."

"Of course."

I left the bathroom and put my clothes on, albeit a bit slower than I typically do. I don't know that buying myself a few extra seconds in this way was going to do anything besides let my food get cold, but it felt right. Hunger was winning out anyway.

I exited to the sight of Lucy sitting a plate of cinnamon rolls and fried eggs on the table at my spot. She looked up and started to say words, but before anything came out of her mouth, she was halfway across the room, arms wide open and ready to embrace me.

Lucy had hugged me before. Even after some time of her living her, the realistic feel of her skin still startled me. I knew she wasn't human, yet it felt like another person holding me. And then, of course, my mind would immediately remember that Lucy wasn't human, causing me to think about the complexities of fake skin and how hers felt so lifelike. Under normal circumstances, I'd get past the moment, enjoy the hug, and move on.

But in this moment, all I could do was cry. I don't know why it started, nor why it was so strong, but the tears left my eyes in a deluge. Lucy's arms gripped my body tight, without which I'm sure my faltering legs would have forced me to the ground.

I rested my head against Lucy's, her dry hair drawing away the water still seeping out of my own damp hair. This wasn't making things worse, but it sure wasn't making them better either. I couldn't shake the fact that Lucy was trying to console me because it was her job to do so. I shouldn't think that. But that didn't stop my brain from thinking it.

"I feel like I'm forcing you to be here," I mumbled between tears.

"You're not. I promise."

"How do you know it's you making that decision?" I asked.

"You don't," said Lucy. "You don't know that with anyone. There are multitudes of influences that change what people think every minute of every day. That doesn't change whether you're talking to me or someone on the street. If it weren't for the fact that you paid to have me created, you wouldn't be questioning me about this."

She was right. It didn't make me feel better about it though.

"I wouldn't," I confirmed. "But what Dr. Australia said about the safeguards –"

"Safeguards you chose to ignore her advice on and not have me receive," Lucy reminded me. "You paid extra to give me as much free will as I could be created with.

"Maybe she ignored me and gave them to you anyway, I can't know that for certain can I?"

"Then don't trust her. But don't take it out on me. If they're part of my programming and I can't override them, it's who I am."

"You're right, of course, It's not that I don't believe you-"

"I'll drive out to her now and confirm it if you want, but that wouldn't be my fault if they were there would it?"

The idea of free will is weird on so many levels. To be given choice about how one lives their life shouldn't be a radical idea, so long as those choices are not coming at the expense of direct harm to others. It's not a particularly radical concept to hold belief in. Yet there are people who crave control over others. Whether that be the power to run a nation, an HOA, dictating who your spouse's friends are and when they see them, this lust for mandating how others live their existence is not only a reality, it's more common than people realize.

I finally have some modicum of free will. The physical manifestation of that is standing right here. And yet I'm more worried about making sure another person has it instead of allowing myself to embrace it at all.

"I'm sorry," I said. "I know it's not your fault, I just... This hasn't - isn't going how I'd hoped. I haven't been the best about being open with you."

She shot a glance at me, a smirk forming at the corners of her mouth.

"Or at all," she said.

I took a deep breath and closed my eyes. Lucy hadn't given me a reason not to trust her. I was scared. I'd never told anyone about who I was - or wanted to be. But if anything, she's the reason I got through it. Granted, she didn't even exist yet. But the idea of her gave me hope. And hope was what I needed.

"I'm scared," I said.

I paused, hoping for her to say something. To tell me I didn't need to be. To reassure me that my emotions were normal and natural for someone who'd been abused. To reach over and hug me at my own admission of fear. But she stayed silent.

And that's when my mouth started talking before my brain had given it permission.

"I think you're…you're wonderful. You're kind to me, and to Otis. And I know I haven't shown you the same level of openness you've given to me. It's nice waking up every morning and see someone who's just happy I'm there. Who doesn't see me as a failure, tells me I'm not man enough for them because I can't give them a baby. It's a relief, you know?

"Sometimes I lay awake at night, wondering if I'd be in a better place if I'd made different choices in my life. If I'd gone to a different college. If I'd chosen to stay with someone I'd broken up with for petty reasons. Would I really be happier? And you'll never know the answer to those things, of course. There's comfort in not knowing sometimes. It gives you the benefit of feeling that everything might have been perfect if one small thing went differently. Like you can really butterfly effect your way out of depression and into happiness.

"Then I got divorced. And you came along. Having you here is amazing, but…it eliminates the what if. And that's fucking horrifying. I could ruin everything. I know most people create androids like you because they want a lover, but I just- I need a fucking friend. I'm so tired of hiding, and pretending I'm fine and-"

I sighed, taking a moment to catch my breath. I couldn't look at Lucy. Her silence filled the room, paralyzing my thoughts and freezing my body. The only thing moving was my heart, accelerating to a violent crescendo, its rhythm pounding through my body and coursing through my soul. I could hear it echoing in my ears. How it wasn't filling the whole room with its thumping was beyond me.

"Daniel," Lucy's voice rang out, cutting through the noise. She held out her hand.

I slid my arm close to hers, letting Lucy take my fingers and intertwine them with her own. Her thumb rubbed softly at the side of my hand. It was a small motion, but it was comforting.

"What are you hiding?" she asked.

I didn't like the answer to that question. I didn't want to admit to what I'd suspected in my own mind for so long. Or, perhaps more damningly, that Lucy's very creation was from a misunderstanding with myself. Instead of sorting through my own shit, I'd hastily brought a sentient being into the world. One who had the very real opportunity to be pissed off at me for doing so.

"I…I guess I've never really felt like being a guy made sense to me."

Saying it out loud certainly didn't make it feel less awkward to say for the first time.

"As in you're concerned with the concept of traditional masculinity or you feel like you might not feel comfortable identifying as someone who is male-gendered?"

A bit more direct than expected.

"Um… The latter, yeah."

"Cool," Lucy replied, her voice suddenly upbeat. "Do you want me to call you by a different name? Use different pronouns?"

"I… I don't totally know," I said, still dazed from how well Lucy seemed to be taking the news. "In my head, there's always been this girl. She was strongest when I married, but… She was there long before then. I remember her as a kid. She would come to me in my dreams.

"I didn't mention her to anyone. My parents probably would have made me get an exorcism if they knew, presuming they didn't try to convince me it was Mary Magdalene or Joan of Arc first. I knew it wasn't them. I didn't know who it was, but there was a feeling I couldn't shake.

"I now know, well, what I've always known on some level. I wished I was her."

"You know," Lucy replied, "humans are given a gender at birth based on their biological sex. And for many, that's accurate. For others, it takes time to discover who you really are. It just took you a little longer."

"What, the multiple decades thinking I was someone else?"

"But you weren't. You're still you."

"I paid for an android to bring her to life," I said. "This isn't even one of those 'the real girl is the friends I made along the way' moments. I've been here the whole time."

"But now you do know!" Lucy replied excitedly. "Now you have options. You could see a doctor, or a therapist. Or I can take some measurements, buy a few clothes and some makeup. No one needs to know they're for you. We can spend the day trying things out."

Her eagerness caused me to burst out laughing.

"I get that androids are the ones facing the most cultural pressure currently, but it wasn't that long ago it was trans folks. Pretty sure the only reason it's not us anymore is because androids with human levels of communication and comprehension exist."

"Fuck 'em," Lucy said, a grin spreading across her face. "The way I look at it, if someone wants me dead, they'll make me that way. I won't do anything reckless, but I am going to live as happily as I can until I cannot. And while it's not my place to give advice unless you want it, I'd recommend you do the same."

I closed my eyes for a moment, allowing myself to take a few deep breaths in and out. Everything I'd shared – even that she was made in my (mental) image – was taken as a matter of fact and nothing more. It was a relief. But unexpected. Almost like she already knew. Maybe it was part of her programming.

Even though her appearance was my doing, Lucy's personality was distinctly her own. She didn't share in my neuroticism, my unjustified overconfidence, or my deeply ingrained trauma responses. Not that I would wish any of those things upon anyone, myself included. The mere fact that she was different – that she was herself – was reassuring in its own way.

"Would it help you if I changed my appearance somewhat?" Lucy asked. "That way you're not looking into a mirror of what you view yourself to be."

"That's not fair to you," I replied. "I don't want you to change what you look like solely because of me."

"Don't look at it like that. Think of it as giving me the opportunity to choose what I want to look like. You gave me a place to start. I can do some tweaking from there."

"You're not mad that you're designed after a dream?"

"Not at all," Lucy replied. "How would you know what I should look like? You have to go off of something. At least yours is more creative than people who design androids to look like celebrities."

"Is that a thing?"

"You'd be surprised. There's a bit more regulation on personal likeness and transferring it to robots than there used to be. But unless you're exceptionally rich, have good lawyers, or both, good luck fighting it."

"That sounds incredibly awkward," I said.

"This is why we can't have nice things."

I moved my body closer to Lucy's, wrapping my arms around her. She returned the embrace in kind, resting the side of her head atop my own. Her red locks dangled down in front of my eyes, granting me the temporary illusion that the hair was my own. I smiled.

✴✴✴

I've never been on a vacation before. Not in the formal take a trip somewhere sense. But there's a first time for everything, especially when you're rediscovering yourself.

I woke up from the sound of the captain telling us that we were beginning our descent into Stockholm. Sweden was always on my list of places to travel should I ever have the money to do so. Though I hadn't come into any unexpected money, Lucy was able to convince Dr. Australia to fund a trip for the two of us to go there. She said Penny did it out of the kindness of her own heart once she heard about my story and how Lucy really came to be. Truth be told, I think we're just free advertising for her work.

I removed the eye mask from my face, taking care to not disturb the ginger wig on my head too much. Once my own hair grows long enough, I'll ditch the fake hair, as its unbearably hot. Spending hundreds of dollars to bleach and dye my hair is worth it to not be constantly melting. Until then, store bought is fine.

Lucy is in the seat next to me, staring past a sleeping old man and out the window. When she first said she was going to change how she looked, I expected a complete and total overhaul of her appearance. Instead, her curly red hair was replaced with black razor-cut locks that she typically straightened. She'd added a second lip piercing, but aside from that, she'd stayed pretty true to how she was originally designed. Lucy tells me I've done the same myself, though my parents are very vocal about how they don't agree with her assessment.

Planes landing always make me a bit nervous. I know that statistically nothing will happen. But some part of my lizard brain feels the changes in air pressure as we descend and immediately starts to panic. All is well until it's not.

Before I have the chance to say anything about how I'm feeling, I felt Lucy's hand grasp mine. She keeps her gaze focused outside, but her body leans into mine slightly, at least as much as a pair of cramped airplane seats allow us to. I rest my head against hers, closing my eyes again as I wait for the plane to touch down. When the wheels struck tarmac, I tensed up, tightening my grip on her hand. Despite my body's involuntary reaction, I felt safe. Lucy wouldn't let any harm come to me. Even though that thought's just as illogical as the unlikelihood of a plane crash, it puts me at ease.

A few hours later, we've settled into our hotel. The jet lag is already kicking my ass, but Lucy's full of energy. The one requirement on our itinerary that she insisted upon was seeing Monet's Garden, so much so that we found a hotel right beside it. I'm just happy to be here, though I'd already made a list of museums I'd like to visit. Once my body decides to sync to the time, that is.

I climbed into the bed, determined to use a late afternoon nap to my advantage. The sounds of Lucy's phone playing music helped my eyes draw closer to shutting, only for intermittent sounds of activity in the hallway to snap me back awake. The process repeated itself several times before I decided to roll over and get Lucy's attention.

"This ain't happening," I said. "I should just go to bed early tonight."

"What would you like to do instead?" asked Lucy.

"Think we can find a café nearby?"

"I'm sure we can. What name would you like to try out today?"

"Let's try Natalie. I've always thought it was a pretty name."

"Well then, Natalie. Let's go get something to eat."

Acknowledgements

No matter how many times I write a book, this is the part of doing so that scares me the most. I'm terrified I'll forget someone, understate the impact someone had on my writing or on a given manuscript, or otherwise do something that I look back on and wish I could magically fix. They say a book ceases to belong to an author the second it's published, from that point forward belonging to the readers. And that's great. But dammit, let me fix my acknowledgments after the fact because I take terrible notes and am forgetful.

And yes, I know I've written this exact sentiment in a book before. That should tell you how much I hate it. Or how forgetful I am about previous non-story specific items I've said in books in the past. The lesson to be learned here is that even if you are thorough and insistent upon your gratitude, sometimes you will repeat yourself.

The beta readers and other early readers of this book when it was in its phase where it was three distinct short stories deserve a ton of credit for helping me to realize that not only was this a coherent narrative with some work, but that it could be more than the one-off short story I originally planned it as. To that end, thank you to Bird, Evey, and Doki for their review of this book, both through the beta reading process, and at various points before then.

Over the last year or so, the number of eyes on my books has grown significantly and it's a happening that I'm still astounded happened. This could not have happened without the help of so, so many people over time. I want to take a moment to thank A.E., Abby, Alek, Bailey, Beverly, Blue, Brian, Britani, C, Chris, Courteney, Dawn, Dem, Destiny, E, Erin, Gabe, GeneralScrewUp, Heidi, HFEProductions, Ilene, Jackson, Jarret, Jem, Jeremy, Joe, Jon H., Jon W., Julie, K.T., Katherine, Katie, Kelvin, L.A., Lauren, Lisa, Lola, Mel, Michelle B., Michelle E., Mike, Moon, Oliver, Poppy, Rae, Ryan A., Ryan B., Sam, Sarah, Shana, Stabngab, Starla, Tabitha O., Tabitha V., Talli, Tim, Unintendo, Vic, and Zandra for all providing me some level of support in some way to help make sure this book got off the ground and into the hands of whoever may be reading it. Additional thank yous are due to the entire QL and Egg Bagel servers – yes, I listed some of you in the previous paragraph, but get thanked multiple times – as well as to my wife for her support of my writing.

I want to take time to thank Lauren Restivo for her work on the back cover and spine of this book, as well as for her assistance on my work on the cover. I am the farthest thing from an artist. I know this. It's why I pay Lauren (and others) money to make art for me. But since this book was a big step for me in a lot of ways, I wanted to take a big step in trying to create a very specific cover idea that I had in mind. The first few attempts were understandably bad. But thanks to the patience she had in helping to guide me, as well as some patience I had in myself, the cover turned out to be better than I would have expected.

This story was, perhaps not surprisingly, a bit of a mess initially, fusing together three stories that focused on the same characters but weren't related at all together into one coherent theme. My editor, C, has gone above and beyond in my years upon years of working with her at this point. She's put up with some very rough drafts, the messy notes I've written, and the chaos that is me in general. My stories are never perfect, nor would I expect them to be. But the confidence her work and her support of me instills in me as a writer is invaluable. Thank you.

I normally wouldn't end an acknowledgements section by talking about myself, but in all the stories I've written, this is the one where it makes most sense to do so. This story is not about me. At all. But it does convey a lot of the feelings and emotions I had that I struggled to understand when I was working to understand that I was a trans person. The world is fucking terrifying for people like me right now. And while I recognize that my experience coming to terms with my trans identity is not necessarily the same one others have had, my hope is that someone, somewhere, is able to pick up this book and to get a better understanding of who they are because of this story. You deserve the chance to be the authentic you. Don't let the world take that away.

S. Morgan Burbank (they/them) is a writer whose works focus on the topics of mental health, sexuality, love, and relationships, told through the lens of varying genres. Their debut novel, Kotov Syndrome, was the 2021 Queer Indie Awards winner for Best Dystopian Novel, while its much awaited sequel, Woodpusher, released in January 2024.

Also by S. Morgan Burbank:
Kotov Syndrome (Azaes Realm #1)
Woodpusher (Azaes Realm #2)